LOVE

FAR FROM BEING FAIR

Dynamo Effect

Manjunatha AR

NOTION PRESS

Published by
Notion Press Media Pvt Ltd,
#7, Red Cross Road,
Egmore, Chennai, Tamil Nadu 600008

Book title: Love Far From Being Fair Vol-1
Subtitle: Dynamo Effect

ISBN XXX-X-XXXXXXX-X-X

First Impression Dec 2023
The moral right of the author has been asserted.
This edition is for sale in the Indian subcontinent only.

Printed in India

Ordering Information
Quantity sales. Special discounts are available on quantity purchases
by corporations, associations, and others. For details, contact the
publisher at the address above.

NOTION PRESS

India. Singapore. Malaysia.

ISBN- XXX-X-XXXXXXX-X-X

Contents

|| Shree Krishnarpanamastu ||

To All

Real-Life Love Stories

Prologue

a love story unfolds in the heart of Mangalore, where the gentle waves of the Arabian Sea meet the shores and spices fill the air. It is a tale of two individuals whose paths cross unexpectedly in a place where destiny weaves its magic——a testament to the enduring strength of love.

Let me introduce you to Arjun, a talented architect whose vision extends far beyond what meets the eye. His architectural creations are not structures; they embody his passion for sustainability and his aspiration to make a lasting impact on the world. However, amidst his blueprints and towering skyscrapers, Arjun yearns for something extraordinary: Love that transcends all boundaries.

Then there's Meera, an Ayurvedic doctor whose healing touch can mend physical bodies and wounded hearts. Her world is steeped in age traditions and ancient wisdom, yet beneath these layers lies an unspoken desire for a love that knows no bounds——a love as boundless as the vast ocean that embraces her hometown.

As fate intertwines their lives on Mangalore's streets, everything changes forever. Love blossoms amidst the chaos——a connection that defies distance, time and societal expectations. This love is also marked by tragedy——a bond tested by fate's harshest trials.

Experience Arjun and Meera's journey as they navigate life's waters. With each passing day, their love story unfolds with separations, reunions and a more robust flame. It is a tale of love that defies fairness, showcases their love's impact on their lives and will touch the hearts of all who believe in the timeless strength of love.

-      **[*Globetrotting_Urban Saint*]**

Place: Vijaynagar, Mysore
Date:28/12/2023

***

"I've seen the other side of love, too, the side filled with fakeness, cheating, and heartbreak. It's a side of love that can make people lose their minds and shatter their trust and faith in love and life itself."

-   A.R

"In the labyrinth of life, where dreams and destinies collide, their love became the compass that guided them through the chaos, illuminating a path of resilience, hope, and the enduring power of the heart."

-   Globetrotting_Urban Saint

Chapter 0

No Comments

****

I wish I had been fifteen minutes late for class that day. It could have saved me five years of hardship, two years of heartache, and three years of depression. But fate had its plans, and as the sun entered Capricorn on Jan 15th after a long hiatus, things were destined to happen as usual. A.R., known for his aversion to crowds and meaningless conversations that yielded nothing, would always make a beeline for his classroom, settling comfortably in the back bench he is bor backbencher, fully absorbed in his world and non-academic pursuits. Engineering had never captured his interest, so skipping internals and classes was his norm.

However, on that fateful day in early January 2019, during his final year of engineering, he arrived at the college twenty minutes early for class. It was 8.05 am when he reached the college and started climbing the steps to the second floor where his class was held. The class was slated to begin at 8.30 am. As he ascended the final steps of the second floor, he absentmindedly glanced up towards the classroom door, and there she was—a breathtakingly beautiful girl.

Standing 5 feet 6 inches tall, with luscious long hair cascading down over her flawless, fair skin, she has thick hair that hangs slightly below her shoulders. Even though her hair looked black, it had a brown shade. She wore oval-shaped spectacles with red-hinged arms resting on her ears and a black oval frame that only added to her charm. Her uniform consisted of a pinkish cream colour top kurta with a round neck paired with a blue churidar and blue dupatta, and she stood at the door with her hands folded, wearing a watch on her left wrist and a red thread on her right. Impeccably groomed and elegantly dressed, she wore sandals that accentuated her graceful legs as she slid to the door.

She caught A.R.'s gaze and smiled at him.

Her eyes are almond-shaped and very dark black with dark eyelashes. She has a broad, square face with a pointed chin. Her nose is short and a little turned up at the end. Her skin is golden-white with a subtle rosy glow around her cheeks. She looked fair and tall and skinny, but she had a slouch that made her look shorter than she was. She always wears simple gold hoop earrings and a couple of silver rings in both hands. She is "pretty" and shy initially, but she opens up a lot once you get to know her. She's astute and has a wicked sense of humour. She has a quiet voice and speaks in a very level tone. Her speech is slow and deliberate, and she always takes a moment to think about what she wants to say before talking. She was a young girl at 22.

Lost in his world, A.R. initially assumed she was smiling at someone behind him and turned around to check, but no one was there.

After a few seconds of confusion, it dawned on him that she had indeed smiled at him. He couldn't fathom why or how, and in utter bewilderment, he walked past her and entered the classroom. It was love at first sight if you are an Indian cinema lover, but rather the spark that ignited a fireworks display in both their hearts. Perhaps she had deliberately chosen to stand there, aware that A.R. was an early arrival to class, or perhaps it was simply a coincidence. Regardless, it marked the beginning of a beautiful two-year relationship intertwined with three years of post-breakup complex challenges, depression, and trauma for A.R.

***`

Chapter 1

Café Serendipity

****

The sun sank below the horizon, painting the city of *Kudla*. (*The Tulu language name "Kudla," meaning "junction", due to its location at the confluence of the Netravati and Gurupura rivers, adds a deeper layer of cultural significance to the city's identity*). *Kudla*, also known as Mangalore, Mangaluru, is a major industrial port city in the Indian state of Karnataka. It is located on the western coast of India, between the Western Ghats in the east and the Arabian Sea in the west.

Mangalore is Karnataka's fourth-largest city and the state's largest coastal city. It's also the headquarters of the Dakshina Kannada district, Known for Its hot and humid weather, Its many beaches and good restaurants and coastal food, Its status as one of India's fastest growing cities, and the most disciplined people known for their brilliance in the banking and education sector.

Mangalore, with a golden glow, the busy streets, alive with the commotion of life, seemed to calm down as the city embraced the arrival of twilight. Amidst places where stories unfolded, Café Serendipity served as a sanctuary for those seeking solace in the delightful scent of freshly brewed coffee and the comforting hum of conversation.

Arjun sat alone at a corner table near the window of the café. Sketchbooks and a steaming cup of coffee partially obscured his slender figure. He exuded an artist's vibe with his tousled hair and casual attire. Behind his glasses, his observant eyes scanned the café's patrons, seemingly searching for inspiration in every passing face. Although Arjun worked as an architect, his passion was capturing life's essence through his art.

Arjun is in his mid 20s
He is 5 feet 6 inches tall and has an air of self-assuredness that matches his vision.
His skin carries a tan, kissed by the sun—a testament to his affinity for spending time and appreciating nature's beauty. Arjun possesses a resonant voice that reflects both his confidence and determination. He possesses a laid-back fashion sense, often seen in well-fitting casual outfits that seamlessly blend with his artistic nature. Arjun is fond of tones and sustainable fashion, which mirrors his dedication to friendly architecture.
On the contrary, Meera, With her flowing hair adorned by a jasmine blossom, her attire that combines tradition and

style and an aura of tranquillity that envelops her like a protective shield, commands attention wherever she goes. As a practitioner, her days revolve around healing and comforting others. However, tonight, she finds herself lost in her thoughts.

Meera is in her mid-20s with a height of around 5 feet 3 inches. She carries herself gracefully with poise. Her skin radiates an olive complexion—a testament to her practices and deep connection with nature. Meera's voice is Gentle, a soothing balm for those seeking solace through her healing touch. She prefers outfits, often opting for traditional Indian clothing infused with modern elements. Her wardrobe showcases colours and natural fabrics—symbolizing her reverence for Ayurveda principles and Indian heritage.

Arjun and Meera's physical attributes, as their style choices, mirror their personalities and worlds. Arjun encompasses the energy of an architect dedicated to design, while Meera radiates the calmness and wisdom of an Ayurvedic practitioner deeply rooted in her cultural heritage. Together, they weave a captivating love tale against the backdrop of Mangalore culture and breathtaking natural landscapes.

The café exudes the scent of brewed coffee, and the soft buzz of conversation sets a cosy atmosphere for this unexpected encounter. Arjun's agile fingers gracefully move across his sketchbook, translating the world surrounding him onto paper with strokes and confident lines. In that moment, he captures the interplay between light and shadow on a vase filled with wildflowers when he senses someone's presence nearby. Meera stands at the café counter, her eyes fixed on the menu board as she ponders her choices. The warm glow from above accentuates her features and subtle undertones in her cinnamon-coloured complexion. She exudes an air of confidence that catches the attention of those around her, infusing an aura of tranquillity into the café.

Arjun's hand pauses midway through his sketch as he watches her intently, entirely captivated by her beauty. He can't. Admire how she looks on her jet-black tresses, creating a halo of shimmering darkness around her. He experienced a thrilling sensation coursing through him—a feeling that something extraordinary would unfold.

When Meera approached the counter, her eyes briefly met Arjuns. It was an interaction. Within that moment, something shifted. Their gazes locked for a fraction of time, and, in that instant, it felt as if time itself had paused. It was as though fate had conspired to bring these two souls into this café on an unremarkable evening.

Meera made up her mind. She ordered a chai latte. As she waited for her drink, she couldn't resist stealing another glance at the man with the sketchbook. There existed a connection between them—a force pulling them closer. She had never felt such an immediate attraction towards a stranger before.

Similarly, Arjun found it impossible to look away from her. He observed as she received her chai latte, cradling the cup. Meera turned around, scanning the café until her gaze eventually settled on Arjun again. This time, their eyes held each other's gaze for moments longer, intensifying their connection further.

Meera gracefully approached a chair at Arjun's table with a subtle, inviting smile.

"Is it alright if I join you?"

She asked, her voice soft and melodic, possessing an effect on the most restless souls.

Momentarily taken aback by her beauty and elegance, Arjun swiftly regained his composure. His heart raced as he gestured towards the chair opposite him.

"Of course ",

he replied warmly, making space for her by sliding his sketchbook.

As Meera settled into the chair, their eyes met more, enveloping them in a warmth. They exchanged introductions, and Arjun discovered that she was named Meera and worked as a doctor. Her deep dedication to the healing system fascinated him. He listened as she shared her work and commitment to helping others find balance and wellness.

In return, Meera found herself captivated by Arjun's soul and his ability to perceive beauty in every aspect of life. She admired his book's sketches, showcasing his perspective on the world as Arjun recounted his travels and expressed his passion for architecture. His realm of creativity and imagination draws Meera.

As they conversed, time seemed to slip while they shared their dreams and aspirations. The cafés atmosphere gradually faded into the background, immersing them in the moment. Arjun's sketchbook lay untouched on the table, forgotten as they delved deeper into each other's lives. Their laughter and engaging discussion created a sense of intimacy amidst the café activity.

As the evening progressed, Arjun and Meera's connection grew more assertive. The initial spark of attraction between them continued to burn, casting an optimistic glow over their serendipitous encounter at Café Serendipity. Little did they realize that this meeting would begin a love story that would challenge and transform them in ways beyond their imagination.

***

Chapter 2

Unexpected Connection.

****

The days that followed their chance encounter at Café Serendipity seemed to pass by filled with messages, phone calls, and stolen glances. Arjun and Meera's connection sparked like a flame in the night. They couldn't ignore the attraction pulling them closer.

On a Saturday afternoon, Arjun stood outside Café Serendipity with a racing heart, a mix of excitement and nervousness consuming him. He had suggested meeting Meera. She had agreed. Today, they planned to explore the streets of Mangalore – a city of hidden treasures just like their blossoming bond.

As he waited for Meera's arrival, Arjun felt a sense of anticipation. The city came alive before his eyes with its facades and bustling markets. He discovered beauty in the designs of buildings, the aroma of spices wafting from street vendors and the mesmerizing array of colours adorning the marketplace.

Finally, he spotted her walking towards him, her face illuminated by a smile. Meera had chosen to wear a saree that blended tradition with grace. Its hues and intricate patterns enhance her natural beauty. Her presence was like a beam of sunshine on that street.

"Arjun!" she called out, her voice filled with affection.

He walked towards her. They embraced each other with a hug, their hearts beating in harmony.

"Meera, you look wonderful."

Arjun complimented his gaze, tracing the contours of her face.

"Thank you "

She replied, blushing slightly.

"You're quite handsome yourself."

With their fingers intertwined, they embarked on a journey through the streets of Mangalore. Arjun guided Meera through alleyways adorned with shops and bustling markets.

He pointed out landmarks and shared captivating tales of the city's cultural heritage. Meera listened attentively, captivated by every word he uttered.

As they strolled through the marketplace, they paused at a street vendor's stall selling handicrafts. Arjun picked up a scarf and handed it to Meera.

"This reminds me of your saree,"

He remarked playfully.

Meera examined the scarf with a sparkle in her eyes.

"Indeed it does! I think I'll take it home as a souvenir."

The vendor, a woman with weathered hands, observed the couple with a knowing smile.

"Ah, love ", she softly murmured, a wistfulness lacing her words.

Both of them blushed without looking at each other.

Their exploration of the city eventually led them to a time-worn temple nestled among coconut trees. The temple's intricate architecture and tranquil surroundings left them spellbound. They settled on the temple's steps, relishing the serenity that enveloped them.

Meera turned towards Arjun. Inquired,

"What is it about architecture that captivates your interest?"

Arjun reclined slightly, his eyes fixed on the ceiling of the temple.

"I believe it's the concept of creating something that can inspire and convey stories without uttering a word. Architecture embodies poetry etched in stone and mortar."

Meera nodded pensively.

"I feel similarly about Ayurveda. It encompasses more than healing one's body; it aims to restore equilibrium and harmony in a person's life. It resembles a symphony of well-being an orchestration."
Their shared dedication to their fields forged a deeper bond between them. They delved into conversations about their

dreams and aspirations, their love for endeavours and their yearning to leave a positive imprint on the world around them. It felt as though their souls were elegantly dancing to a rhythm, each step drawing them closer together.

Arjun suggested they visit an art exhibition as the day shifted to evening, creating quite a buzz in the city. Meera readily. Together, they made their way to the venue of the exhibition.

The art gallery is filled with various colours, each painting telling its unique story. Arjun's eyes sparkled with admiration as he took in the canvases, while Meera appreciated the beauty and emotion expressed through every brushstroke. They strolled through the gallery hand in hand, sharing their thoughts and interpretations of the artwork they encountered.

One particular painting captured their attention—a breathtaking masterpiece depicting a landscape bathed in the hues of sunset. Arjun found himself irresistibly drawn to it, sensing a significance hidden within its colours and scene.

Meera stood beside him, her gaze fixated on the painting.

"It's awe-inspiring" she whispered.

Arjun turned towards her, his eyes filled with intensity.

" like you," he uttered tenderly.

Their gazes. Within that moment, surrounded by art reflecting their blossoming connection, Arjun and Meera shared their first kiss—a gentle exchange of emotions sealing their growing affection.

The art gallery, filled with masterpieces, seemed to hold its breath as they separated from their kiss, their hearts beating in sync.

Arjun and Meera's fingers remained intertwined as they exited the exhibition, symbolizing their commitment to embark on this journey. The lively streets of Mangalore had witnessed the birth of a love story that surpassed all expectations and embraced the unexpected.

Under the night sky and amidst the pulsating rhythm of the city, Arjun and Meera delved deeper into the enigmas of their bond. They understood that every shared moment was like a canvas waiting to be adorned with the hues of their affection.

22

***

Chapter 3

Love Blossoms

****

The weeks they were passed by. Arjun and Meera's bond grew more assertive with each passing day. Their love blossomed gradually like a flower, revealing its beauty. Mangalore's streets and vibrant atmosphere became the backdrop for their enchanting love story.

On a Friday afternoon, Arjun stood outside Café Serendipity, his gaze scanning the streets of Hampankatta. It had become their tradition to meet in the city's heart near the Clock Tower circle. The clock tower held more significance than being a landmark; it symbolized the passage of time. Arjun couldn't Feel that every second spent with Meera was a treasure he cherished as each tick resonated through his being.

Meera arrived, her steps quickening as she caught sight of Arjun. Her smile exuded warmth. Her eyes sparkled with excitement as she approached him. The vibrant energy of the Clock Tower circle seemed to reflect their joy.

"Arjun ", she greeted him melodically.

He welcomed her with a kiss on her cheek and his fingers lightly brushing against hers.

"Meera, you become more beautiful every time I look at you."

Her cheeks turned a shade, a blush creeping across her face.

"You're quite the wordsmith, Arjun."

As they embarked on their walk through the bustling streets, Arjun reached out. Naturally, he intertwined his fingers with Meeras like two puzzle pieces fitting together perfectly. It was a gesture. It held deep significance—a wordless acknowledgement of their growing affection.

The Clock Tower circle buzzed with activity. Vendors peddled an array of flowers, fruits and fragrant spices, creating a symphony of senses that enveloped them. Arjun guided Meera to a flower stall where he carefully handpicked a bouquet of jasmine blossoms, knowing they were her favourite. With a smile, he presented them to her as she inhaled their fragrance, and her eyes sparkled with delight.

"Thank you "

She expressed her gratitude.

"You have a way of making every moment feel special."

Arjun's eyes locked onto Meera's gaze. Within that shared look, they understood the connection between them—a connection that surpassed mere words; it was an unspoken promise of love and devotion.

Their exploration of Hampankatta continued as they delved into the cuisine—indulging in street food delicacies and quenching their thirst with coconut water. Arjun couldn't. Admire how effortlessly Meera blended into the city's fabric, attracting admiring glances with her elegance and grace.

They decided to explore a bookstore nestled amidst the Clock Tower circle. Arjun's eyes lit up as he perused the shelves filled with novels, art books and timeless classics. Knowing his love for literature, Meera watched him with a smile, her heart swelling with affection.

Arjun selected a Novel, **Abachurina Post Office,** by *K.P Poornachandra Tejaswi* and Handed it over to Meera.

"I thought you might appreciate this," he said.

Gratefully, Meera accepted the book.

"Thank you, Arjun. It's such a gesture."

Hours flew by as they engaged in animated conversations about their books, beloved authors and the incredible power of words in expressing emotions. The clock above them ticked away, marking time's passage. They felt like time paused within that bookstore sanctuary—almost like the universe conspired to grant them cherished moments together.

As evening approached, Arjun proposed they visit an art gallery nearby. Mangalore's flourishing art scene had become an area of shared interest for them both; They eagerly embraced the chance to immerse themselves in the realm of creativity. The art gallery, a treasure on the street, showcased a captivating blend of contemporary and traditional artwork. The walls were adorned with paintings reflecting the artist's passion and unique vision. Arjun and Meera strolled hand, in hand immersing themselves in the colours and heartfelt emotions captured on each canvas.

Amongst the array of artwork, they stumbled upon a mesmerizing painting that seemed to mirror their journey. The masterpiece portrayed a couple standing beneath a night sky, their hands delicately entwined to express their love. Arjun and Meera exchanged a knowing glance, feeling a connection to the emotions evoked by the artistry.

As they stood before this captivating painting, Arjun whispered,

"It's as though the artist has beautifully encapsulated our souls."

Meera smiled serenely, her gaze fixated on the artwork.

"Love is a language that transcends boundaries, Arjun – it knows no limits of time or place."
In that tender moment shared between them, they sealed their love with a kiss amidst the ambience that enveloped them. The gallery witnessed the depth of their affection while the universe seemingly rejoiced in harmony with their union.

Leaving this enchanting gallery behind them, they gazed up at the night sky shimmering with stars – it was as if nature was celebrating their love in splendour. The Clock Tower circle, in Hampankatta, with its presence, stood as a guardian to their growing fondness. Their journey was far from complete. As they strolled hand in hand through the bustling streets of Hampankatta, Arjun and Meera understood that their love story was commencing. Each step they took and each moment they shared served as a testament to the splendour of love. A love that wasn't perfect held a charm unlike anything they had experienced.

***

Chapter 4

Hurdles

****

As the weeks turned into months, Arjun and Meera faced a juggling act, trying to balance their demanding careers with their blooming love for each other. The challenges of nurturing their relationship and ambitions were becoming increasingly evident.

Arjun stood in front of his apartment mirror at the crack of dawn, straightening his tie and taking a breath. Today, he presented at Urban360 Private Limited, the architecture firm where he was employed. The anticipation surrounding his design proposal for a residential complex in Mangalore was mounting, adding to his felt pressure.

Meera also encountered obstacles at SDM Ayurveda Hospital in Bejai, Mangalore. As a doctor, her days were often filled with an unending stream of patients seeking holistic healing. The ancient practice of Ayurveda demanded her focus and commitment. She took her role as a healer with utmost seriousness.

Their careers brought them fulfilment and satisfaction. It also cast shadows on their relationship. Navigating through deadlines and intricacies specific to their professions became hurdles they had to overcome

One evening at Café Serendipity. Their cherished spot. Arjun and Meera found themselves cloaked in silence that weighed heavily between them.

Arjun's mind was consumed with thoughts of designs and project deadlines, while Meera focused on reviewing files and ensuring their well-being.

Breaking the silence, Arjun expressed his frustration with a hint of regret.

"Meera, I apologize for being so preoccupied lately. This architecture project has taken up all my time."

Understanding his situation, Meera nodded empathetically.

"I understand, Arjun. I've also been occupied with my responsibilities at the hospital... I can't. Miss our quality time together."

As they sat across from each other at the table, their hands naturally sought each other's touch, interlocking like puzzle pieces. It was a gesture that conveyed emotions.

Arjun confessed softly,

"I miss it too. Our leisurely walks through Hampankatta, our visits to art galleries and those quiet moments we shared at the bookstore."

Meera smiled wistfully, her heart filled with longing for those moments.

"Arjun, our love is strong like a lotus that thrives in waters. We need to find a balance between our careers and our relationship."

Arjun gently squeezed her hand with determination shining in his eyes as they faced the challenge together.

"You're right, Meera. We can't allow our careers to overshadow the bond we share. Let's work together to find that harmony."

So Arjun and Meera embarked on a journey to discover the equilibrium between their deep love for each other and their passion for their professions. They were determined to make it succeed.

Arjun began implementing boundaries at Urban360 Private Limited.

He designated time slots for meetings and design tasks, ensuring that he could devote quality time to being with

Meera. He also started working from home, allowing himself to be closer to her.

Meera, too, adjusted her schedule at SDM Ayurveda Hospital. She tried to efficiently complete her responsibilities, freeing up more time for her patients and herself. She realized that taking care of her well-being was crucial to continue providing care for others.

One evening after a day at work, Meera arrived at Arjun's apartment with a delightful surprise—a homemade dinner. The delightful aroma of spices filled the air as she lovingly set the table with dishes she had prepared herself.

Her gesture deeply moved Arjun—the effort she had put into preparing the meal.

"Meera, this is wonderful."

"You didn't have to go through all this trouble," he said gratefully.

A warm smile graced her face as she presented him with a plate of biryani. "Arjun, I want us to have moments like this where we can unwind and enjoy each other's company."

As they relished the meal together, the pressures and worries of their day seemed to dissolve into the air. Laughter filled the room as they exchanged stories, rediscovering the delight of being in each other's presence.

Their weekends became a haven—a time when they could escape from the demands of their careers and fully immerse themselves in one another world. They ventured to Mangalore's beaches, finding solace in the sound of waves crashing against the shore and the gentle caress of the sea breeze on their skin.

One Sunday, they ventured into Mangalore's outskirts, following winding roads through breathtaking landscapes. Eventually, they found themselves at the foot of a hill with a sunset that painted hues across the sky.

Hand in hand, they ascended towards the summit of that hilltop while witnessing how gracefully the sun descended below the horizon. Mesmerized by the beauty unfolding before his eyes, Arjun turned towards Meera, his gaze reflecting appreciation.

"Meera, no matter how hectic our lives may become, I want to be by your side—sharing moments like these."

Meera felt a surge of love as she leaned in to kiss him.

"Arjun, our love is like the sea's ebb and flow—it may go through ups and downs. It always comes back stronger than ever."

Their dedication to each other and determination to balance their lives with their love story started yielding results. It wasn't always sailing. They learned to cherish their moments together, whether stealing a lunch break, having late-night phone conversations, or going on weekend trips.

Arjun's architectural designs continued to thrive, earning him recognition and praise at Urban360 Private Limited. Meeras Ayurveda's practice flourished as she found fulfilment in helping her patients achieve well-being and harmony.

One evening, Arjun received an invitation from Meera. She had arranged for them to attend an art exhibition reminiscent of where they shared their kiss. It was a testament to the effort they were investing in nurturing their love amidst the challenges of their careers.

As they gazed at a captivating painting in the art gallery—an image depicting two hearts intertwined amidst the world's chaos—they realized their love had endured its share of challenges and storms. However, like the hearts in the artwork, their love remained resilient and unwavering, a testament to the strength of their bond.

With each passing day transforming into months, Arjun and Meera's love story unfolded further, with each chapter showcasing their dedication to one another. They discovered that love wasn't always equitable; it presented its set of hurdles and obstacles. Yet it was through facing these challenges that their love grew more assertive. The Clock Tower circle at Hampankatta bore witness to the stages of their romance. Now, it stood as a symbol of their resilience—a love that had endured times test and emerged more beautiful and enduring. So Arjun and Meera embarked on their journey together—a love story far from perfect but filled with hope for a future where their affection would thrive amidst life's trials and triumphs.

***

Chapter 5

After Six Months

****

Arjun and Meera had encountered obstacles together. The impending storm on the horizon would put their love to the ultimate test. While navigating the complexities of their lives, a fresh set of challenges arose, threatening to pull them.

Arjun and Meera had planned to enjoy some quality time in the ambience of Mangalore's evening. Arjun had just returned from presenting his eco-resort design proposal at Urban360 Private Limited, which received approval. Meanwhile, Meera had spent a week at SDM Ayurveda Hospital attending to patients with health conditions.

They opted for an escape to a beach on the city's outskirts; it was a place they had visited before. The rhythmic crashing of waves against the shore provided a comforting soundtrack as they engaged in conversation. These moments of respite became precious to them as they could genuinely be themselves away from work pressures.

Sitting side by side on a weathered driftwood log and witnessing the sun descending below the horizon, Arjun turned towards Meera with a mix of pride and concern in his eyes.

"Meera ", he began,
"I am overjoyed about my design being approved. It also means I'll have to travel frequently for this project."

"There's a lot of work ahead, and it might mean we'll have to put in hours ", Meera acknowledged, understanding the demands of Arjun's career. However, down she couldn't. Feel a tinge of sadness at the thought of their precious time together being further reduced. She looked out at the expanse of the sea. Spoke softly but determinedly.

"Arjun, I fully support your dreams and ambitions because success means a lot to me.. I don't want us to lose sight of what we have." Reaching out for her hand, Arjun intertwined his fingers with hers.

"Meera, I don't want that either. I promise we'll find a way to balance everything and make it work."

Their unspoken commitment to each other was accentuated by the call of seagulls above them, as if even nature bore witness to their vow.

Arjun's project at Urban360 Private Limited gained momentum, making his trips more frequent. He often found himself working late into the night, meticulously examining blueprints and designs. His pressure was unrelenting, leaving him torn between his flourishing career and his profound Love for Meera.

At the time, Meera also encountered challenges in her role at the hospital. A sudden influx of patients had placed a burden on her demanding schedule. She frequently worked hours with unwavering dedication towards Ayurveda principles. The pressure of their jobs started affecting their relationship as they spent less time together.

One evening, while sitting at Café Serendipity, the weight of their circumstances seemed to hang in the air. Arjun ran his fingers through his hair, frustration evident in his voice. "Meera, I feel like this project is consuming me. I can barely think, let's have quality time with you."

Meera's eyes filled with understanding as she reached across the table to touch his hand. "Arjun, I know how important your career is to you. We can't let it overshadow everything. We need to find a way to strike a balance."

Arjun nodded wearily, his shoulders slumping under the weight of exhaustion. "I understand that, Meera. I don't want us to lose what we have. You mean everything to me."

She gently squeezed his hand and spoke softly. "And you mean everything to me, too, Arjun. We'll find a way through this together."

So began their journey towards restoring harmony in their lives. Arjun realized the toll his demanding job took on their relationship and started delegating tasks at Urban360 Private Limited. They both learned the importance of setting boundaries and managing their time wisely. Meera also made some adjustments to her hospital schedule by seeking assistance from a trusted colleague, allowing her to have time for herself and for Arjun.

One day, they decided to revisit the beach where they had made their promise to each other. The clear sky and endless sea brought a sense of tranquillity to Arjun, making his heart feel lighter than it had in weeks.

Beside him, Meera nestled close, resting her head on his shoulder. "Arjun, I'm so proud of you for prioritizing our relationship by changing your career," she said warmly.

He gently kissed her head and expressed his gratitude, "Meera, you mean everything to me. I don't want us to lose what we have because of my aspirations."

A renewed sense of hope enveloped their hearts as they watched the sunset. They knew challenges would arise along their journey together but believed their love was resilient enough to withstand any storm.

Arjun and Meera's relationship began stabilizing with the passing months as they found balance and harmony. They treasured their moments together, more fully aware of the preciousness of their time amidst their demanding careers. Their love had been tested; It grew stronger, akin to steel forged in the fires of adversity.

Arjun was nearing the completion of his project at Urban360 Private Limited, which meant he travelled frequently. Meera's responsibilities at the hospital had also lightened, giving her flexibility in her schedule. It felt as if fate had conspired to grant them a break, an opportunity to reignite their love.

One evening, as they sat on the beach more with the setting sun enveloping them in its glow, Arjun reached for Meera's hand and looked deeply into her eyes.

"Meera, I promise always to prioritize our time together no matter how busy life is. Our love is truly paramount to me."

She smiled warmly, her heart brimming with affection. "Arjun, I make that promise to you. Our love is a treasure that shall never fade away."

With renewed determination and a heightened sense of gratitude for their shared love, Arjun and Meera continued on their journey together. They were aware that life would always present obstacles. They were also aware that their love, like a guiding lighthouse in waters, would always bring them back to one another.

The Clock Tower circle at Hampankatta, which had witnessed the ups and downs of their relationship, now stood as a symbol of their enduring love. This love had faced its share of challenges but emerged more resilient and exquisite than ever before.

So with the promise of a future and a love that had weathered the storm, Arjun and Meera continued to script their love story—one enriched by experience fortified by commitment and carried by an unwavering belief that their love was far, from perfect but undeniably the most beautiful they had ever known.

***

Chapter 6

New Horizons

****

As the love story between Arjun and Meera unfolded, they found themselves on the brink of a chapter in their lives. Both of them were facing twists. Turns in their journeys, challenging them professionally and as deeply loving partners.

Arjun had always nurtured a passion for architecture. However, his recent accomplishments at Urban360 Private Limited have opened doors to opportunities. One morning, he received a call from an international architectural firm offering him a chance to work on a groundbreaking project in Singapore. This opportunity held potential for career growth and global recognition.

Meera also reached a point in her career at SDM Ayurveda Hospital. Her unwavering dedication to her practice allowed her to lead a research project on integrating Ayurveda with Western medicine. It was an endeavour that had the potential to revolutionize healthcare in India.

Sitting together at Café Serendipity, their spot for introspection and heartfelt conversations, Arjun brought up the topic with excitement and apprehension.

"Meera,"

He said hesitantly, "I've been offered an opportunity to work on a project in Singapore—a project that could be transformative for my career. It would mean relocating for years."Meera's eyes widened in surprise as a mix of happiness for Arjun's success and concern for their relationship flooded her heart. "Arjun, this is Great. I'm genuinely proud of you. What does it mean for us?"

Arjun reached out to hold her hand, his expression filled with sincerity. "Meera, you mean the world to me. I don't want to lose you. At the time, I can't let go of this opportunity."

Meera nodded thoughtfully, her fingers intertwined with his.

"Arjun, I want you to pursue your dreams. I'll be by your side every step of the way. Even if it means being apart for some time, we can make it work."

Their commitment to prioritizing each other's dreams and aspirations demonstrated the strength of their love. They understood that this new chapter in their lives would present challenges they hadn't anticipated before but were determined to face them.

Arjun accepted the offer from the firm, and preparations for his move to Singapore began earnestly. The idea of a long-distance relationship weighed heavily on their hearts. They were resolute in making it work.

Before Arjun left, he and Meera had a day exploring the city of Mangalore one last time. They revisited the Clock Tower circle at Hampankatta, where their love story began. The iconic landmark seemed significant that day, bidding farewell to one chapter of their journey and welcoming what lay ahead.

Their city exploration was filled with laughter and cherished memories. They stopped by the art gallery where they shared their first kiss and strolled along Tannirbhavi Beach, Surathkal Beach, Panambur Beach, Ullal Beach and especially Panambur Beach — each holding its special meaning in their hearts. They also visited a sapna book house that held value for them.

As the day ended, they found themselves atop a hillside where they had once watched a sunset together. Arjun held Meera close.

"Meera, no matter how far apart we may be physically, you will always reside in my heart."

Tears welled up in Meera's eyes as she gazed into his eyes. "Arjun, I will patiently await the day destiny brings us together again."Their farewell embrace, beneath the twinkling stars, overflowing with affection, yearning and hoping for a future where their love would again unite and flourish.

Arjun's journey to Singapore was laden with both obstacles and opportunities. He fully immersed himself in his project, dedicating effort to making his mark in architecture. Meanwhile, in Mangalore, Meera focused on her research endeavour, finding fulfilment in her work and the satisfaction of contributing to healthcare advancements.

Despite the distance that separated them, Arjun and Meera made unwavering efforts to stay connected. Regular video calls became their routine as they shared stories of their lives and aspirations for what lay. The time difference between

India and Singapore posed its challenges. Their love remained a source of strength.

One evening, as Arjun gazed out from his apartment window at the shimmering Singapore skyline, a sense of longing washed over him. Overwhelmed by his emotions, he reached for his phone and dialled Meera's number with a racing heart.

Meera's face appeared on the screen—her smile radiating warmth. "Arjun ", she greeted eagerly. "How is everything in Singapore?"

He let out a yearning sigh before responding, "Singapore is truly incredible, Meera—but it feels incomplete without you."Meera's eyes glistened with emotion, reflecting the feelings as his own. "I think about you every day, Arjun. I'm incredibly proud of everything you're accomplishing."

Despite being challenged by the distance between them, their love remained unwavering. They both understood that their respective careers were leading them on paths for a purpose, and they were determined to make the most out of this time.

Months turned into a year. Arjun's architectural project in Singapore was nearing its completion. He had achieved success in his field. His heart yearned for the day he could return to Mangalore and reunite with Meera.

Meera's research project at SDM Ayurveda Hospital also yielded results, earning her medical recognition. Her professional journey was thriving; however, she eagerly awaited their reunion.

On a day in Singapore, Arjun found himself standing on the rooftop of a towering skyscraper admiring the sprawling cityscape before him when an unexpected phone call came through. It was an invitation to speak at an architecture conference in Mangalore—an opportunity to showcase his work and share his experiences with aspiring architects.

Arjun's heart filled with exhilaration as he accepted the invitation. It meant going to the city he adored, reuniting with Meera and bringing their dreams of togetherness closer to reality.

As the conference date drew near, Arjun's excitement intensified. He knew this visit would be a moment in their relationship—a chance to reassess their priorities and decide their future.

Meera, too, eagerly awaited Arjun's return. The thought of seeing him again stirred a mix of excitement and nervousness within her. Their love had endured time and distance. They both understood that they couldn't be indefinitely.

The day of Arjun's arrival in Mangalore, she was brimmed with anticipation. Meera stood at the Mangalore International Airport, Bajpe, her heart racing as she observed passengers disembarking from the plane. Then she spotted him—the presence of Arjun striding toward her with a smile capable of illuminating even the darkest night.

***

Chapter 7

Reunion

****

Arjun had eagerly counted down the days, hours and minutes until this moment arrived when he would finally lay eyes on Meera again. It felt like an eternity since he last embraced her, and the longing in his heart had grown into an ache, a reminder of the love that bound them together.

Stepping off the plane at Mangalore International Airport, a wave of familiarity washed over him as his senses absorbed the surroundings. The refreshing scent of the sea breeze combined with the warmth of the air and the gentle buzz of activity in the airport created a feeling of returning home. Mangalore was where their love story began, and it was here that Arjun hoped to reignite their connection.

Excitement coursed through Arjun's veins as he navigated through the airport, each step bringing him closer to the awaited reunion.

Memories flooded his mind—moments shared with Meera in this place, their encounter, stolen glances exchanged between them and stolen kisses that set ablaze their love.

As he turned a corner, she stood amidst the crowd, eyes scanning for arriving passengers. Seeing Meera's smile and how her eyes lit up when they locked with his was like a soothing salve for his soul. A surge of emotions washed over him—relief, joy and an enduring love that seemed to know no bounds.

As they closed the distance between them, time appeared to slow down. Arjun's heart raced with anticipation, his steps quickening. When they finally stood face to face, it felt as if the rest of the world had faded into insignificance, leaving the two of them.

Meera enveloped Arjun in her arms, their embrace brimming with the warmth of their love. He held her close and buried his face in the softness of her hair.

"Meera ",

He whispered into her ear, his voice filled with love and trembling with emotion.

"I've missed you deeply."

Tears of happiness streamed down Meera's cheeks as she clung tightly to him.

"Arjun, I've missed you too,"

She confessed softly, struggling to find words to capture her longing.

"Being apart has been incredibly tough."

Their lips met in a kiss that conveyed longing, passion and the profound love that had sustained them through months of separation.

The kiss sparked a flame within them that had never truly faded. Instead, they grew more assertive with each passing day they were apart.

As they pulled back from the kiss, their foreheads gently touched each other. Their breaths intertwined. Arjun looked into Meera's eyes with tenderness and love shining in his own.

"Meera, you mean more to me than anything in this world. Being away from you has been the most difficult thing I've ever experienced."

Meera smiled through her tears, her heart overflowing with love.

"Arjun, I feel the way about you more than words can convey... I promise you we will find a way to make this work. Our love is too powerful to let anything come between us."

With their hands entwined, they left the airport ready to embrace all the days and nights ahead of them. Arjun's conference in Mangalore marked the beginning of their reunion. They have marked the start of an incredible journey together that would reignite their passion and deepen their love.

In the following days, Arjun and Meera were inseparable. Each moment became a celebration of their love and an opportunity to rediscover their shared connection.
They wandered through the streets of Mangalore, revisiting the places that held significance for them—the coffee shop where they had their first cup together, the painting gallery

where their first kiss took place, and the beach where they whispered promises of forever.

One evening, as they stood hand in hand on the beach's shores, witnessing a sunset with shades of orange and pink painting the sky, Arjun turned towards Meera. His voice carried a tenderness that he had never revealed before. "Meera, being away from you has made me realize how much you truly mean to me and how essential your presence is in my life. I cannot envision a future without you by my side."

Meera's heart swelled with love and gratitude. She had experienced emotions throughout their time apart, so hearing Arjun openly express his feelings was a relief.

"Arjun, every day we've been apart has only reinforced those sentiments within me. You're not my love but my soulmate—the one I want to share every moment with."

Arjun's eyes shimmered with tears of joy. He gently held Meera's face in his hands. He tenderly kissed her, a kiss filled with love, longing and the unbreakable bond that had grown even stronger during their time.

Their reunion was marked by these moments—moments of passion, tenderness and shared aspirations. It was a period for them to reconfirm their dedication to one another, promising that their love would always prevail regardless of the obstacles they may encounter in the future.

As the days went by, Arjun's conference came to a close. His stay in Mangalore continued. He had reached a decision that would bridge the distance between them and allow them to construct a life together. He chose to relocate to Mangalore to be with Meera and ensure their love would no longer be strained by the miles separating them.

Meera was filled with joy upon hearing Arjun's choice. Together, they searched for a home in Mangalore—where they could lay down roots for their shared future. The Clock Tower circle at Hampankatta stood tall as an emblem of their enduring commitment, having silently witnessed chapters of their love story.

One night, Arjun and Meera stood in front of the clock tower with the stars shining in the sky. Arjun turned towards Meera, his voice filled with certainty. "Meera, our love has been tested time and time again. It has proven to be true. I want to spend the rest of my life with you, building a future filled with dreams, passion and an unwavering love that has brought us together."

Meera's eyes sparkled with joy as she nodded her head.

"Arjun, I couldn't ask for anything more. I love you wholeheartedly. I am eagerly anticipating to create our future."

With intertwined hands, they walked away from the clock tower, ready to embrace whatever lies ahead. Their reunion was a testament to the power of love—of yearning—and of a bond that had reunited them.

As they ventured into the night, their love story continued—a tale woven with passion and longing—a love destined to endure, a love that had weathered separations storm and emerged more vital—more profound—and unshakeable than before.

***

Chapter 8

Building a Life Together

****

Arjun's choice to relocate to Mangalore marked a turning point in his love story with Meera. It was a decision based on their commitment to each other, a commitment that had endured the challenges of separation and only grew stronger. As they began creating a life, they knew that obstacles lay ahead. Their love acted as a guiding light through any storm.

The quest for a home in Mangalore became an adventure they embarked on together. Arjun and Meera spent their weekends exploring neighbourhoods, visiting properties and envisioning their side-by-side. This process brought them closer than ever as they dreamed about the life they would build within the walls of their abode.

On one afternoon, they stood before a bungalow nestled amidst coconut trees. The salty fragrance of the sea filled the air while distant waves crashing created a soothing melody. Arjun turned to Meera with eyes. Asked,

"Meera, what are your thoughts about this place?"

Meera gazed at the bungalow adorned with tiled roofs and white walls emanating charm. A smile spread across her face as excitement overwhelmed her heart. She replied to Arjun, saying,

"Arjun, it's perfect."It feels like a place where we can make memories."

With that choice made, they focused on personalizing the bungalow. They selected colours, furniture and decorations that reflected their shared style. Gradually, the bungalow transformed into a welcoming home—a sanctuary where their love would thrive.

As they settled into their life together, Arjun and Meera embraced the joys and challenges of living under one roof. They discovered each other's quirks and routines, sharing laughter and finding compromises. It was a period of adjustment that only deepened their connection, affirming their compatibility.

Arjun transitioned his career to Mangalore by leveraging his expertise to contribute to the city's development. His passion for architecture perfectly aligned with Mangalore's commitment to eco-innovative design. He gained recognition in the community, and his designs began embellishing the cityscape.

Meanwhile, Meera poured her heart and soul into nurturing the wellness centre in SDM, which had become a haven for individuals seeking healing and equilibrium. The centre's reputation flourished, attracting people from all corners of India who sought Ayurveda wisdom and tranquillity through practices.

Meera's dreams of impacting people's lives were finally coming true as her vision became a reality.

While excelling in their careers, Meera and Arjun consciously prioritized their relationship. They established rituals to nurture their connection—a dedicated date night every week, leisurely morning walks along the beach, and quiet moments of reflection in their garden. The clock tower at Hampankatta stood tall as a symbol of the enduring strength of their love.

One evening, as they wandered through the streets of Mangalore, Arjun turned to Meera with a sparkle in his eyes. "Meera, I've been working on a project that resonates with you. It's an eco-sustainable community centre here in

Mangalore. I would love to collaborate with you on incorporating wellness into its design. "Meera's heart filled with pride and admiration. "Arjun, that idea is incredible! I would be honoured to join forces with you on this project—it beautifully combines our passions."

Their collaboration on the community centre became a labour of love—an embodiment of their shared vision for creating a world.

Arjun and Meera's architectural brilliance seamlessly merged with Meeras's expertise, resulting in a practical and spiritually uplifting design.

The community centre quickly gained renown not for its groundbreaking design but for its comprehensive programs. It became a hub for individuals seeking emotional and spiritual well-being, representing Arjun and Meera's dedication to impacting their community.

Over the years, Arjun and Meera's love story continued to unfold. Their shared aspirations had transformed into reality. They celebrated their accomplishments with humility and gratitude. They recognized that their love extended beyond happiness; it encompassed the potential to influence the world around them positively.

One evening beneath the starry night sky, as they sat together in their garden, Meera turned towards Arjun with contentment in her voice. "Arjun, our love has brought us to this place—a place where we not only build our lives together but also make a meaningful difference in the lives of others."

Arjun beamed with eyes reflecting his Love for Meera.

"Meera, you are my inspiration. Together, we have created something that will leave a lasting impact on the world."

Their love bloomed like a maintained garden thriving with each passing season. It was a love that had faced the challenges of distance and life's uncertainties and emerged even stronger and more resilient. Their love was rooted in dreams and promises. It had stood the test of time because they honoured those commitments daily.

On an evening by the clock tower in Hampankatta, surrounded by the city of Mangalore, Arjun turned towards Meera with deep affection and gratitude in his voice. "Meera, our love story is proof of the power of dreams, the strength found in promises made and the unwavering nature of love. I wouldn't want it anyway."

Meera nestled closer to Arjun's, embracing her heart overflowing with love. "Arjun, our love is a masterpiece—a work of art that continues to evolve and inspire."

Arjun and Meera continued scripting their enduring tale with the clock tower as their witness, a story filled with resilience and eternal as Mangalore itself.

***

Chapter 9

Weathering the Storm

****

Arjun and Meera had built a life in Mangalore filled with love, shared dreams and accomplishments. They created a home, established a community centre and embraced a joyful existence. However, as the saying goes, life is not without its challenges. Little did they know that the path ahead would put their love to the test.

Meera was going about her work at the wellness centre on a summer morning when her phone rang. Seeing her brother Rohan's name on the caller's I.D., she picked up with a smile, assuming it was another routine conversation.

As Rohan's voice quivered with urgency at the end of the line, Meera's heart sank. There had been an accident. Their parents were en route to visit them when they were involved in a car crash. Both of them were now hospitalized with injuries. They were undergoing emergency surgery.

The weight of this news crushed Meera's spirit as she struggled to comprehend what she had just heard.

Overwhelmed by emotions and tears welling up in her eyes, she hung up the phone while her world felt like it was crumbling around her.

Arjun, who had just finished a meeting, hurried to Meera's side when he noticed the distress in her eyes. She shared the news with him, her voice trembling with emotion. Arjun embraced her tightly, feeling the weight of concern in his heart. "Meera, let's go to the hospital away. We'll be there for them. Together, they'll overcome this."

Upon reaching the hospital, they discovered Rohan waiting anxiously in the hallway, his face drained of colour. He provided updates on their parent's conditions – facing a journey towards recovery. Meera's parents had always been pillars of strength and support; witnessing them in such a state was heartbreaking.

Arjun and Meera took turns staying by their parents' side at the hospital, offering solace and ensuring they received top-notch care. Days turned into weeks as their parents underwent surgeries, physical therapy sessions and rehabilitation programs. Amidst managing their responsibilities at the wellness and community centres, Arjun and Meera made the hospital feel like their home.

The stress and emotional strain of the situation began to take its toll on both Arjun and Meera. Nights became restless as worry consumed their thoughts.

Meera's parents had always been a source of strength. Witnessing their pain served as a reminder of how fragile life can be.

One evening, in the lit living room of their bungalow, Arjun turned towards Meera with concern in his eyes. "Meera, I can see how deeply this is affecting you. You have been juggling work, the wellness centre and being there for your parents. Remember, you don't have to bear the world's weight on your shoulders."

Feeling exhausted, Meera let out a sigh. Her fatigue weighed down her shoulders. "Arjun, I can't. Feel responsible. If my parents hadn't been coming here to visit us when the accident occurred, they wouldn't be going through this ordeal."

Arjun gently held Meera's face in his hands. He made her look into his eyes. "Meera, you are not at fault for what happened. Accidents happen beyond our control. Your parents would want you to care for yourself and continue pursuing your dreams."

Touched by Arjun's words and gesture, tears welled in Meera's eyes as she leaned into his touch.

"I understand how difficult it is to see them in this state, and I want to do everything to assist in their recovery ", Meera expressed with a heart.

Arjun nodded empathetically. "We will overcome this together, Meera. Lean on me, lean on all of us. We have a support system, including Rohan and our friends, ready to lend a hand. You don't have to bear this burden."

In the following weeks, Meera gradually started accepting the help and support from those around her. She entrusted some of her responsibilities at the wellness centre to her team members while Arjun took on tasks at the community centre. This truly showcased the strength and deep love of their partnership.

As time passed, it became evident that the accident had left lasting effects on Meera's parent's health. Her father, full of vigour and vitality, now faced mobility challenges. Her mother, an embodiment of grace and resilience, experienced moments of frustration as she coped with emotional pain.

Meera and Arjun's love story gained depth as they stood by her parent's side during their recovery journey.

They dedicated hours to research and consulted with experts to ensure Meera's parents received the possible care and therapy. In return, Meera's parents sincerely appreciated the love and commitment shown by their daughter and designated son-in-law.

One evening, while sitting in the garden with Meera and Kalyani, Meera's mother turned to Arjun with tears in her eyes. "Arjun, we are incredibly grateful to have you by Meera's side. You've been our rock throughout all of this."

Arjun smiled warmly, touched by Kalyani's words. "Aunty, it is an honour for me to be a part of your family. Meera is my Love. I will always be there for her and both of you."

Kalyani reached out. She gently held Arjun's hand as she looked at him with gratitude. "Both of you have faced challenges together. Your love has only grown stronger. It truly demonstrates your commitment to one another."

Rajesh Meera's father, who had been silently listening, nodded approvingly. "Arjun, you and Meera have built a life together. We are incredibly proud of both of you."

The storm that entered their lives tested their love and resilience.

Meera and Arjun had gone through it all, emerging with a bond and a deeper connection. It served as a reminder that love's not just about the times; it's also about standing together when faced with challenges.

As time went by, Meera's parents continued to make progress in their recovery. They celebrated victories – the steps, regained strength and moments of shared laughter that filled their home. Meera and Arjun were there to witness each milestone, their love unwavering and their commitment unbreakable.

One evening, while standing in front of the Hampankatta clock tower with the city of Mangalore surrounding them, Meera turned to Arjun. She expressed her gratitude. "Arjun, this storm has tested us in ways we never anticipated. It has also revealed our love's depth and ability to face challenges together."

With a squeeze of Meera's hand, Arjun conveyed his love from within his heart. "Meera, our love is a wellspring of strength that will carry us through whatever obstacles life throws us. We have weathered the storm. Emerged on the side even stronger."Under the gaze of the clock tower, Arjun and Meera embarked on a journey of love—a tale showcasing their unwavering strength, their ability to stand united in the face of challenges and a bond that nothing could break. Their love had weathered storms as a testament to their dedication and unyielding connection.

***

Chapter 10

Dreams Realized

****

Arjun and Meera had faced a period in their relationship where They overcame it and grew even more vital as Meera's parents continued to recover, and life returned to a rhythm. Their days were filled with love, shared aspirations and an unwavering belief that they could overcome any obstacles that crossed their path.

One beautiful morning, while sitting together in their garden and enjoying cups of chai, Meera's mind wandered to a dream she had cherished for a time. With a sparkle in her eyes, she turned to Arjun. "Arjun, do you remember when we first met? I shared my vision of creating a wellness retreat where people worldwide could find healing and balance."

Arjun smiled warmly as he remembered the moment vividly. " course, Meera. It was your passion and your dreams that attracted me to you."

Meera's voice grew more determined as she continued speaking. "Well, Arjun, it's time for us to realize that dream. Considering our success with the wellness centre and community centre projects, I truly believe we can create a wellness retreat that offers our guests a transformative experience."

Excitement ignited in Arjun's eyes as he eagerly responded. He always admired Meera's mindset and ability to turn dreams into reality. "Meera count me in completely. Let's make your dream come true."

With their decision finalized, Arjun and Meera adventured to bring their dream of a wellness retreat to life. They dedicated themselves wholeheartedly to the project, combining Meera's expertise in healing with Arjun's architectural skills.

They searched for the location. They discovered it an untouched piece of land surrounded by nature, adorned with lush forests and offering breathtaking views of a tranquil lake. The site's beauty was a canvas to manifest their healing and personal transformation vision.

Designing the retreat became an endeavour fueled by passion. Arjun prioritized principles incorporating eco-friendly materials and energy-efficient designs to be integrated with the natural environment. Meera ensured that every element of the retreat exuded a sense of harmony, from the gardens to meditation spaces.

As construction commenced, Arjun and Meera encountered their share of obstacles. Delays, budget constraints and inevitable setbacks accompanied such an undertaking. Their love and determination carried them through every obstacle. They pushed forward with unwavering determination.

One evening, while standing on the construction site and witnessing the retreat taking shape, Arjun turned to Meera, feeling pride in his heart. "Meera, just look at what we're building. It's more than a retreat; it's a place of healing, transformation and love."

Meera nodded appreciatively, her eyes brimming with gratitude. "Arjun, this reflects our shared dreams and commitment to impacting the world. I couldn't have asked for a partner on this journey."

The holistic wellness retreat quickly gained attention and anticipation within the community and beyond. People were drawn to the concept of a sanctuary that offered healing and nurtured spiritual and emotional well-being. The retreat's mission was to provide individuals with a space to reconnect with themselves and find balance in the world.

As the opening day of the retreat approached, Arjun and Meera devoted themselves tirelessly to ensuring that every detail was flawless. They trained a team of therapists and healers, curated wellness programs meticulously and crafted spaces that exuded tranquillity and serenity. The clock tower in Hampankatta reminded them of their journey, filled with love and the fulfilment of dreams.

The day they finally arrived for the opening of the retreat. It was indeed a momentous occasion. Friends, family, well-wishers and esteemed guests celebrated Arjun and Meera's achievement. The retreat's doors were opened wide, welcoming guests worldwide to embark on their journeys of healing and self-discovery.

Standing before the crowd, Meera couldn't. Feel overwhelmed with emotion as she spoke. "Today marks the realization of a dream we have nurtured for years—a dream centred around healing, transformation and love. We cordially invite each of you to experience this place's enchantment; discover balance within yourselves and reconnect with your essence."

An electric sense of excitement filled the air as Meera concluded her speech. The retreat's opening proved to be a success as guests from around the globe began arriving. Their purpose was clear—to seek solace, rejuvenation and a deeper connection with their selves. Arjun and Meera couldn't. They swell with pride as they witness lives being transformed within the tranquil walls of their retreat.

However, this particular day held another surprise in store. Mr. A.R., the CEO of Urban360 Private Limited, arrived as the chief guest for the ribbon-cutting ceremony. Mr. A.R. Wasn't only an entrepreneur but a local legend—a symbol of resilience and personal growth.

In Mangalore, Mr. A.R.'s name was synonymous with dedication and achievement. However, what truly made him stand out wasn't his business skills but his remarkable journey of self-improvement. He was renowned for his transformation and ability to bounce back after experiencing a heart-wrenching love failure.

Years ago, Mr. A.R. faced a setback that left him shattered. It was a love story that captivated the city—a whirlwind romance ending abruptly, leaving Mr. A.R. Emotionally devastated. His heartbreak had an impact on his professional life, leading many to believe he would never fully recover.

Inside, Mr. A.R.'s resilience prevailed against all odds. He possessed a determination and an inner strength that few were aware of. Instead of succumbing to despair, he confronted his demons head-on by finding solace in his work and immersing himself in his role as the CEO of Urban360 Private Limited. Under his guidance, the company had witnessed a growth surge. Mr. A.R.s unwavering commitment to excellence has transformed Urban360 into a thriving architecture and real estate force. His passion for architecture and innovative design garnered the admiration of his peers and the city.

Yet it wasn't solely his achievements that made Mr. A.R. A hero figure. It was his transformation. He embarked on a journey of self-discovery, immersing himself in literature, philosophy and spirituality. Seeking guidance from mentors and therapists, he was determined to heal the scars left by his experiences. It finally took three years to become normal. After a series of medications and meditation, **he overcame depression and Hypertension. It took three years of his prime time.**

As he addressed the gathering at Arjun and Meeras wellness retreat, Mr. A.R.'s confidence radiated subtly strongly. His journey from heartache to triumph became a beacon of hope for many in Mangalore. He exemplified that during life's moments, one can summon the strength to rise above adversity and rebuild one's life with greater resilience.

Mr A.R.s speech commenced with an acknowledgement of the significance of this day;

"I am honoured to be present here, at this retreat's inauguration—a place that embodies healing powers and transformative potential."
He commended Arjun and Meera for their approach and unwavering commitment.

As Mr A.R. Continued speaking, he shared his experiences encompassing love, life and work. His words served as a testament to the significance of perseverance in the face of challenges. He emphasized the influence of love as a source of inspiration. He has also stressed the importance of balancing growth and professional achievements.

"Love possesses power ",

declared Mr. A.R., his voice filled with conviction and high spirit.

"However, it should not be our driving force. We must discover our strength to forge ahead when love encounters obstacles. We can attain greatness through our resilience and unwavering determination."

His speech deeply resonated with the audience, many of whom had followed his journey from heartbreak to success. They saw Mr A.R. not only as a CEO but also as an inspiring figure—a hero who had gracefully confronted adversity and emerged as a symbol of hope.

Mr. A.R. said, I Repeat.

"Love is a powerful force, But it's not the only".

After his speech, Mr. A.R. Received a standing ovation. Attendees approached him with gratitude, sharing their stories of difficulties and resilience. His visit impacted the retreat's atmosphere, infusing it with a renewed sense of purpose and determination.

Arjun and Meera were deeply moved by Mr. A.R.s words and their positive influence on their guests. They realized that their retreat was not merely a place for healing but a space for emotional and spiritual growth. It served as a haven where individuals sought to reconnect with themselves and find the strength to overcome life's trials.

Concluding the tape-cutting ceremony, Arjun, Meera and Mr. A.R stood side by side with their hands joined together, representing unity and triumph. It was a moment that symbolized more than the beginning of a retreat.
It represented the fulfilment of dreams, the strength of love and the unbreakable spirit of those who dared to overcome their challenges.

As they stood in front of the clock tower at Hampankatta amidst the city of Mangalore, Arjun, Meera, and Mr A.R. Understood that their journeys were far from complete. They were bound together not by the ceremony of cutting the tape but by their shared belief that anything could be achieved with determination, resilience, and the support of loved ones.

****

Chapter 11

A Difficult Decision

****

---

6 Months Later

"Meera " Arjun started, his voice filled with uncertainty

"We need to have a conversation."

Meera met his gaze, her eyes mirroring his apprehension.

"Arjun, I've noticed it too. There's something we can't keep avoiding."

They had been evading the issue for weeks, unable to face the decision ahead. This decision held the potential to alter the trajectory of their journey. Its weight burdened their hearts. As they settled on a bench beneath the shade of a sprawling tree, Arjun clasped Meera's hand in his own.

"Meera, we've created something here—a place of healing, love and transformation. It also comes with responsibilities that demand our dedication."

Meera nodded silently, her gaze fixed on the ground below.

"Arjun, our retreat has become a sanctuary for souls. We've impacted our guest's lives; we can't simply abandon that."

Arjun gently squeezed her hand while expressing understanding in his voice.

"I understand, Meera. However, we must also consider our well-being and future.

"The retreat has been demanding, consuming much of our time and energy. Although it has been a fulfilling journey, it has left us room for ourselves and our aspirations. Tears welled up in Meera's eyes as she spoke.

"Arjun, I've cherished every moment of this journey. I can't ignore the toll it has taken on us. We have made sacrifices for the retreat. Is it wrong to desire something for ourselves?"

Arjun's heart ached as he gazed at Meera, the woman he loved more than anything.

"Meera wanting more is not selfish; it's only human. We deserve a life beyond being defined by the retreat — a life where we can pursue our dreams and passions."

Their conversation lingered in the air like a cloud of uncertainty and doubt. The decision they were facing carried weight – a pivotal moment that would shape their future together. They had to find a way to balance their love for the retreat with their love for each other and forge ahead with an approach that honoured both aspects.

In the following days, Arjun and Meera sought comfort in their routines. Found solace within the supportive community of the retreat.

However, the choice they faced continued to burden their minds, a reminder of the moment they had come to.

One evening, while sitting in their office, Meera broke the silence. "Arjun, we can't keep avoiding this. We must make a decision that allows us to strike a balance between our love for the retreat and our longing for a life of our own."

Arjun nodded, his eyes fixed on the calendar hanging on the wall—the calendar that had witnessed every step of their journey from the beginning. "Meera, I agree. It's time we engage in a truthful conversation about the future of the retreat and what it means for us."

With their decision, Arjun and Meera resolved to gather their core team from the retreat for an honest discussion. They sought to hear perspectives and insights from those who had shaped its journey—an expedition that had touched lives.

As the team assembled in the hall, Arjun and Meera initiated dialogue. "We've accomplished something here ", Arjun began with confidence in his voice.

"This retreat has become a place of solace and growth, which speaks volumes about the dedication and hard work put in by everyone involved."

Meera continued her words resonating with emotion. "However, it also comes with a responsibility that has consumed a part of our lives. We have invested our hearts and souls into this retreat, witnessing its impact on our guests."

The team members listened attentively, their faces reflecting curiosity and concern. They sensed something was unfolding. We're eager to grasp Arjun and Meera's intended path.

Arjun addressed them more, his gaze sweeping across the room. "Meera and I have engaged in conversations about the future of this retreat, leading us to arrive at a decision. We believe it is time for us to step away from our day-to-day involvement."

Meera added, "This is not a choice we have made lightly. We hold affection for this retreat and its principles; however, we must also prioritize our well-being and pursue our dreams and passions."

Silence filled the room—a weight that hung heavily in the air.

The team members exchanged glances, taking in the significance of Arjun and Meeras' announcement. The retreat had been a vision, an effort, so the news of Arjun and Meera stepping back evoked mixed emotions.

Ramesh, one of the team members, cleared his throat.

"Arjun Meera, we understand that this decision must have been tough for both of you. We've witnessed your dedication and passion for this retreat. However, we also recognize the importance of balance and self-care."

Priya, another member of the team, nodded in agreement. "We've all been deeply moved by the retreat mission. We've witnessed how it has positively transformed our guests' lives. Above all else, we genuinely care about your happiness and well-being."

Arjun and Meera felt grateful for their team's understanding and support. They shared a moment of vulnerability—a moment where they all acknowledged that the retreat had transcended being a business venture; it had become an endeavour driven by love and provided immense fulfilment. As they continued discussing matters, they devised a plan to ensure a transition.

Arjun and Meera gradually transitioned from their day-to-day roles, entrusting team members who shared their passion and vision for the retreat with the responsibilities they had carried for so long. They carefully managed this process, placing importance on the retreat's and its founders' well-being.

In the weeks, Arjun and Meera went on handing over their duties to their team members. It was a mixture of emotions filled with moments of reminiscing and contemplation.

One evening, while strolling through the retreat gardens, Meera turned to Arjun with an expression in her eyes.

"Arjun, it's not a decision to relinquish control. I also sense a feeling of relief. We're taking a step towards finding equilibrium in our lives."Arjun smiled warmly as his heart overflowed with love.

"Meera, our love has always been our guiding force throughout this journey. This decision is founded on our understanding of what it means for us and the retreat."Their choice to step back marked a moment in their story that allowed them to prioritize their well-being and aspirations while ensuring continuous growth and impact for the retreat.

It was a choice filled with emotions and a sense of uncertainty. However, in the end, it had to be made.

***

Chapter 12

Separation Again

****

The retreat had entered a phase characterized by change and transition. Arjun and Meera's decision to step back from their day-to-day responsibilities had initiated a chapter in the retreat's journey. It was a mix of emotions with both excitement and apprehension.

As they delegated their tasks to trusted team members, Arjun and Meera found themselves with time. They used this freedom to pursue their passions and dreams, which had been put on hold for the sake of the retreat.

Arjun, who has always been passionate about architecture and design, engaged in a new project—a sustainable housing initiative to provide affordable and eco-friendly homes to underprivileged communities in Mangalore. This project strongly aligned with his values. He dedicated his energy towards its realization.

On the other hand, Meera rediscovered her love for Ayurveda and holistic healing. She started offering consultations and workshops based on her experience and knowledge. It was an enriching endeavour that allowed her to connect with individuals on a level while guiding them along their healing journeys.

Despite the purpose and excitement they experienced in their pursuits, an undeniable sense of pain and longing permeated their days. The retreat had held a place in their lives for such a time, and now they faced the harsh reality of being separated again.

One evening, as they sat together in their garden, the weight of their choice hung heavily in the air. Meera spoke first, her voice filled with vulnerability. "Arjun, I can't. Feel a longing for the retreat—the daily routines, the connections we forged with our guests and the sense of meaning it brought into our lives."

Arjun nodded in agreement, his own heart burdened by yearning. "Meera, I miss it too. The retreat was more than a business venture; it represented an extension of ourselves— a manifestation of our shared aspirations and core values."

Meera reached out to hold Arjun's hand, their fingers intertwining. "Arjun, I'm proud of what we accomplished.

It also required sacrifices that prevented us from pursuing our dreams and passions."

Arjun gently squeezed her hand as he looked at her with love shining in his eyes. "Meera, our decision wasn't easy to make. It was necessary."We needed to strike a balance in our lives to follow our dreams while supporting the retreat from a distance."

As they conversed, the pain of being separated was tangible as a reminder of their love for each other and the retreat they had jointly established. They were well aware that their decision was the one. It didn't make enduring the separation any more straightforward.

In the weeks, as Arjun immersed himself in his housing project and Meera continued her work in Ayurveda, their lives assumed a new rhythm. They tried to spend quality time together, cherishing those moments when their paths crossed.

One evening, while sitting in their garden as the sun descended below the horizon, Meera spoke softly. "Arjun, I can't, even though we pursue our dreams individually. I feel an emptiness. The retreat was more than a location; it embodied our shared love and purpose."

Arjun nodded as he carried the sentiment within his heart. "Meera, I completely understand. The retreat was a part of who we are. Being separated from it has left us with an undeniable void. However, we cannot allow that void to define us. "We must seek purpose and fulfilment in our endeavours."

As they grappled with the anguish of being, they found solace in shared moments. The love that had sustained them through all their trials. They understood that their love possessed the power to bridge the gap between them as it was responsible for bringing them together initially.

One night, while sitting on the porch under the sky, Meera turned to Arjun with a tender voice. "Arjun, I want you to know that even though we are distant from the retreat, my affection for you and what we have built together remains unwavering."

Arjun smiled, his eyes reflecting affection. "Meera, I feel the way. Our love and shared aspirations are at the core of everything we pursue. Though physically separated from the retreat, our hearts remain intertwined with it and with each other."

Their love served as a lifeline—a wellspring of strength that carried them through the pain of separation. It served as a reminder that their decision, though challenging, was a step towards attaining harmony in their lives and pursuing their dreams.

As time passed and days turned into weeks, Arjun and Meera saw their pursuits flourish. Arjun's sustainable housing project gained momentum, while Meera's private consultations and workshops started gaining a following. They found fulfilment in their passions as the retreat thrived under the care of their team.

One evening, they sat together in their garden, feeling a sense of contentment. Meera expressed her gratitude with a voice of appreciation. "Arjun deciding to step back from the retreat was not easy. However, it has allowed us to pursue our dreams and balance life."

Arjun nodded affectionately, his heart overflowing with love. "Meera, our journey is far from over. Even though we are physically distant from the retreat, our love and shared dreams continue to guide us."

Their separation became a chapter in their story. They also demonstrated the strength of their love and commitment to maintaining balance in life. It was a chapter marked by growth, fulfilment and an unwavering belief that their love could bridge any distance, no matter how great.

***

Chapter 13

Climactic Reunion

****

The retreat was bathed in the setting sun's colours, creating an atmosphere for this special occasion. Arjun had been at the retreat for days, overseeing the preparations for a surprise event that would mark a significant milestone in his and Meera's love story.

As the guests gathered in the garden, their faces filled with anticipation, Arjun's heart raced with excitement and nervousness. The event was meant to surprise Meera, bringing them back to the place where their love had initially blossomed.

News had spread among the retreat team. Everyone had joined forces to make it an unforgettable evening. Arjun collaborated with the retreat staff to create an ambience adorned with twinkling fairy lights, flickering candles and a path strewn with flower petals leading up to a beautifully decorated gazebo.

As the sun disappeared below the horizon, casting a glow over the garden through lanterns and filling it with animated chatter, Arjun anxiously awaited Meera's arrival. His heart thumped in his chest as he sensed that this perfect moment was about to unfold. As if orchestrated by destiny itself. When he caught sight of a car approaching, Meera's car arrived at the retreat. Arjun could barely contain his excitement. He positioned himself near the pavilion, feeling his heart race as he observed her step out of the car.

Meera glanced around, her eyes widening in surprise at the scene before her. The garden, illuminated by twinkling lights, seemed plucked out of a fairy tale. With a growing sense of wonder, she followed the trail of flower petals, each step quickening her heartbeat.

Reaching the pavilion, Meera locked eyes with Arjun. At that moment, everything else faded into the background. She couldn't. Gasp in astonishment at his presence — standing amidst the gentle glow of lanterns with a playful smile.

Arjun extended his hand. Spoke softly with deep emotion in his voice.
"Meera ", he said tenderly, "welcome to our evening."

Tears shimmered in Meera's eyes as she took his hand and spoke with a quiver in her voice. "Arjun, I can't believe you've arranged all this."

They stood together inside the pavilion, surrounded by flickering candlelight and fragrant blooming flowers; it felt like time had frozen for them. Their love story had led them to this moment that held the promise of an awaited and emotionally charged reunion.

As they embraced, their hearts beat in sync, their love for each other surpassing the need for words. It was a reunion that had been anticipated for a time, culminating in all the obstacles and separations they had endured.

Meera pulled her eyes back slightly, searching Arjuns with a blend of affection and yearning. "Arjun, this is... It's more incredible than anything I could have imagined. My heart is filled with joy because of you."

Arjun smiled, his gaze locked with Meeras, his love for her shining. "Meera, every second we've been apart has served as a reminder of our profound love. It's a force that transcends distance and time itself—a force that has brought us back together."

Their reunion stood as proof of the strength of their love—
a love that had endured the trials of time and separation. It
was a love that had only grown stronger through every
challenge they faced.

As they walked away from the pavilion, hand in hand, Meera
couldn't. Smile through her tears. "Arjun, I've missed you
every moment we were apart."I've missed this place, our
retreat and the joy of being with you."

Arjun gently squeezed her hand, determination shining in
his eyes. "Meera, I've missed you too. Our love and
everything that defines us as a couple has been absent from
my life. Being apart has made me realize how much you
mean to me."

Their reunion was a moment, the culmination of a love story
marked by numerous challenges and periods of separation.
It was a juncture filled with hope for a shared future where
their love could again flourish.

In the following weeks, Arjun and Meera continued to revel
in the warmth of their reunion. They knew their journey was
far from over; they still had obstacles and dreams to pursue.

However, they faced it all with unwavering determination, knowing their love could conquer any adversity.

One evening, as they sat on the porch under a sky adorned with twinkling stars casting a glow, Meera spoke softly. "Arjun, our love story has been a voyage filled with ups and downs. It has also catalyzed growth and self-discovery. "I wouldn't change a moment of it, " Arjun said, nodding with pride and deep affection. "Meera, our love has been the driving force behind all our accomplishments. It's been the guiding light that has helped us navigate through every challenge and celebrate every triumph. I wouldn't trade our love for anything in this world."

Their love possessed a strength that transcended distance and time, bringing them together and allowing them to relish in the ecstasy of their reunion. This profound love would continue to shape their journey as a source of inspiration and upliftment.

Arjun and Meera were acutely aware that their love story was far from concluding as they looked towards their shared future. It was a tale woven with passion, dreams and an unyielding belief in the power of love to conquer all obstacles.

Their reunion marked the pages of this new chapter in their remarkable narrative. One brimming with adventure fervour and the enduring strength of their unwavering bond.

***

Chapter 14

Closure and Acceptance

****

The retreat had thrived in the months after Arjun and Meera's reunion. It had become a sanctuary for those seeking balance and comfort, a place where architecture and holistic healing existed in harmony. Amidst the peacefulness, Arjun and Meera discovered a place of their own—a space where they could finally find closure and acceptance.

One evening, as they sat on the porch, the stars above casting a glow, Arjun spoke softly. "Meera, our love story has been filled with ups and downs. It has also been a journey of growth and self-discovery. I wouldn't change any moment of it."

Meera nodded, her heart overflowing with gratitude and love. "Arjun, our love has been the driving force behind everything we have accomplished. It has guided us through every challenge and triumph. I wouldn't trade our love for anything in this world."

Their love was a force that defied distance and time; it had brought them together to experience the joy of reuniting in such an intense way. It was a love that had evolved, growing more substantial with each passing day—a love that had shaped their journey and would shape their future.

Looking towards their future together, Arjun and Meera knew their love story was far from reaching its conclusion. It embodied a tale of love, aspirations and an unwavering belief in the conquering power of love. Their reunion marked the beginning of a chapter in their love story that held the promise of adventure, passion and the enduring strength of their affection.

Over time, they discovered how to harmonize their shared dreams with their aspirations. The retreat they had established became a testament to their love and unified vision—a sanctuary where others could discover solace and find inspiration.

One evening, as they strolled through the gardens of the retreat with contemplative steps, Meera spoke softly. "Arjun, I've been reflecting on our journey—the obstacles we've overcome, the separations we've endured and the love that has sustained us throughout. It's been quite a ride."

Arjun nodded while gazing deeply into Meera's eyes—his love for her radiating. "Meera, our love story attests to our resilience and unwavering commitment. It has been a voyage of growth—exploring finding harmony between our affection and cherished dreams."

Meera smiled warmly as her heart overflowed with joy.
As the retreat thrived, Arjun and Meera dedicated themselves to their passions. Meeras Ayurveda practice flourished, while Arjun's architectural projects gained recognition for their designs.

On a tranquil evening, a sense of contentment filled the air as they sat together on the porch. Arjun expressed his gratitude, his voice resonating with appreciation. "Meera, I take pride in what we've built: the retreat, love and the life we're shaping."

Meera nodded affectionately, her eyes gleaming with love. "Arjun, our love has been the bedrock of all our accomplishments. It is a force that has brought us together and allowed us to find closure and acceptance."
Their love story had completed its circle—a voyage marked by trials, separations and reunions. It had been a journey of

growth and self-discovery that ultimately led them to a place of resolution and embracing reality.

One evening, in the pavilion where they had reunited years ago, Arjun spoke tenderly."Meera, this place holds cherished memories for us—the sheer delight of our reunion, the aspirations we've nurtured, and the deep affection that has sustained us."

Meera's face lit up with a loving smile. "Arjun symbolizes our voyage, a journey that has brought us solace and understanding. Our love has surpassed time and distance; it's a love that will forever be our guiding light."

As Arjun and Meera gazed upon the garden bathed in the radiance of lanterns and filled with the scent of blossoming flowers, they felt a profound sense of resolution.

Their love story was proof of adaptability. In those tranquil moments of the evening when they held each other tightly, Arjun and Meera knew their love story was far from reaching its conclusion. It was a tale woven with love, aspirations and an unshakeable belief in love conquering power.

Their journey had led them to a place where closure intertwined with acceptance—a realm where their love could prosper and inspire generations.

***

Chapter 15

The Dynamo Effect

****

In the quiet moments of the evening, as they held each other close, Arjun and Meera knew their love story was far from over. It was a story of love, dreams, and the unwavering belief that love could conquer all. Their journey had led them to a place of closure and acceptance, where their love could flourish and inspire others for generations to come.

But it was also a story that carried a powerful message—that love, though a force of immense strength, was not the only force that shaped their lives. It was a force that worked with resilience, determination, and the capacity to overcome challenges. It was a force that, when harnessed with unwavering belief, could create a Dynamo Effect—a force that could transform not only their lives but the lives of those around them.

As they stood there, gazing out at the retreat they had built together, Arjun and Meera knew that their love story would continue to evolve, inspire, and make a difference in the lives of others.

It was a story that would live on, a story of love being fair and the enduring power of their love.

And as they looked ahead to the future, they did so with hearts full of love, dreams that knew no bounds, and the knowledge that their love was indeed a force to be reckoned with—a force that could create a Dynamo Effect, a force that could change the world.

***

Epilogue

Years have flown by since the encounter of Arjun and Meera on the bustling streets of Mangalore. Their extraordinary love story has impacted their lives and those around them. The sanctuary they painstakingly built side by side is a testament to their affection, a place where healing, transformation and inspiration intertwine.

As Arjun and Meera find solace on the retreat porch gazing at the shimmering stars in the night sky, they are enveloped by the love that has guided them through every hurdle and triumph. Their love is more than a force; it is a legacy—an enduring symbol of resilience, determination and an unwavering belief in love's inherent strength.

However, their reflections are not moments. A guest who played a role in their journey is accompanying them—Mr. A.R. is the CEO of Urban360 Private Limited. He is known for his efforts, personal growth and profound insights into matters of love and life.

With warm eyes brimming with wisdom, Mr. A.R. Smiles at Arjun and Meera. "Your captivating love story has constantly reminded me of one truth—Love possesses power ", he affirms gently. ". It is solely responsible for propelling us. "Arjun and Meera both agree with Mr A.R.'s words, understanding the impact of love they have experienced. They acknowledge that love is a force that transcends boundaries and transforms lives. However, they also recognize that life is a blend of emotions, dreams and challenges, with love being one element in this intricate tapestry.

As they gaze up at the sky, Mr. A.R. Further explains his statement. He emphasizes that love is the binding force that brings people together, ignites creativity within us and provides strength during times. Nevertheless, he emphasizes that our determination, resilience and unwavering belief in our dreams propel us forward.

Arjun and Meera exchange smiles filled with gratitude for the wisdom shared by Mr A.R. They understand that his love story has been shaped by tragedy but has also been a journey of growth, self-discovery, and unwavering faith in the power of self.

Now, as they observe the garden illuminated by gentle lantern light and adorned with blooming flowers creating an enchanting fragrance around them, Arjun and Meera are aware that their unique tale of love will continue to inspire and uplift future generations. It's a narrative about love, aspirations and the unwavering belief that love can conquer all. However, it also acknowledges the influences that shape our lives.

Underneath the starry night sky, they hold each other close with hearts filled with love and dreams that know no limits. They understand that their love possesses a strength—a power that has sparked a Dynamo Effect that is transforming their lives and touching those around them.

Looking towards the future, they realize their journey is far from complete. It explores the complexities of love, life and the driving forces within us. Their love story isn't a tale; it stands as a testament to the enduring resilience of the human spirit—a spirit fueled by love and so much more.

***

The current success rate in love is 0.1%. Get ready to experience The Prime side of love filled with fakeness, cheating, and heartbreak. It's a side of love most of them get to experience. Let's meet A.R. Once Again in the Upcoming Volume.

We will meet in Volume 2.............

With appreciation and optimism

[Globetrotting_Urban Saint]

Available on Amazon worldwide.

Share Your Thoughts

manjunatha_a.r	
Manjunatha A.R	
Manjunatha A R	
Manjunatha_A_R	
manjunatha_a_r	
Manjunatha_AR	

www.ingramcontent.com/pod-product-compliance
Lightning Source LLC
Chambersburg PA
CBHW022023150726
47990CB00002B/792